the CRiTTeR club

:paw: **Marion's Got the Butterflies** :paw:

by Callie Barkley :heart: illustrated by Tracy Bishop

LITTLE SIMON

New York London Toronto Sydney New Delhi

LITTLE SIMON

An imprint of Simon & Schuster Children's Publishing Division · 1230 Avenue of the Americas, New York, New York 10020 · First Little Simon paperback edition June 2022. Copyright © 2022 by Simon & Schuster, Inc. All rights reserved, including the right of reproduction in whole or in part in any form.

LITTLE SIMON is a registered trademark of Simon & Schuster, Inc., and associated colophon is a trademark of Simon & Schuster, Inc. For information about special discounts for bulk purchases, please contact Simon & Schuster Special Sales at 1-866-506-1949 or business@simonandschuster.com.

The Simon & Schuster Speakers Bureau can bring authors to your live event. For more information or to book an event contact the Simon & Schuster Speakers Bureau at 1-866-248-3049 or visit our website at www.simonspeakers.com.

Designed by Brittany Fetcho

The text of this book was set in ITC Stone Informal Std.

Manufactured in the United States of America 0422 MTN. 10 9 8 7 6 5 4 3 2 1

Cataloging-in-Publication Data is available for this title from the Library of Congress.

ISBN 978-1-6659-1372-0 (hc)

ISBN 978-1-6659-1371-3 (pbk)

ISBN 978-1-6659-1373-7 (ebook)

Table of Contents

M Is for Milkweed

Marion Ballard was searching for a plant whose name starts with the letter C.

She was on the Santa Vista Nature Walk. Her friends, Liz, Amy, and Ellie, followed, their feet crunching on the gravel path. They were playing the Plant Alphabet Game.

"Coneflower!" Liz cried out. She pointed at a purple bloom swaying in the breeze.

Marion turned to face Liz. "Also E for *echinacea!*" Marion said. "That's its scientific name."

"No fair," said Ellie with a frown. "Marion remembers all the science-y names."

Marion smiled. She did enjoy flexing her knowledge sometimes. She remembered a lot from when they had helped to create this Nature Walk.

It hadn't always looked this nice. This part of the park had been overgrown and unused. Once it was almost replaced by a shopping center! Then Marion and the girls found milkweed in the park. They learned it was an important plant for pollinators. So they asked Mayor Gomez and the town council to build the stores somewhere else. And they listened!

Marion, Liz, Amy, and Ellie had made a list of all the plants that grew in the park. Mayor Gomez had educational signs made for each kind. They now dotted the path of the Nature Walk.

"Look!" cried Marion. The path led them past a big patch of milkweed. The flowers were in full bloom. Bees were buzzing all around. Marion even spotted a couple of butterflies.

Amy breathed in. "I can smell it from here!" she said with a smile.

Marion sniffed. A sweet, spicy honey scent filled the air.

At the same time, she was scanning the area for a D plant. "Daffodil!" she called out. "And F for fern," she said, pointing to some plants growing in the shade of a tree.

Ellie sighed in frustration.

When the girls finished the Nature Walk, they were stuck on the letter J. But they were back where they started, and it was time to go home. Amy's and Liz's bikes were parked in the bike rack. Marion and Ellie were getting picked up by Marion's mom.

Beekeeping!

Native Plants Workshop

Butterfly Release at the Arboretum!

Come learn about the importance of monarch butterflies.

Composting with Worms!

While the girls waited, they checked out the park info board. A flyer decorated with butterflies caught Marion's eye.

"Oh!" Marion said. "Gabby and I went to the ladybug release last year. It was so fun. Well, for me it was. A ladybug landed on Gabby's head, and she ran in circles, yelling, 'Get it off!'"

Marion did not get her sister. Why was she so afraid of a tiny bug, smaller than her fingernail?

Unlike Gabby, Marion was used to all kinds of wildlife, thanks to The Critter Club. That was the animal rescue center Marion and her friends had started. The girls had taken care of dogs and cats and goldfish. But also a turtle, a pig, and chickens. Once they even helped a boy find his lost chinchilla!

"Maybe Gabby would like a butterfly release better than a ladybug
one," Amy suggested.

"Less of a crawly critter," said
Liz.

"More of a fluttery flier," Ellie
added.

"Maybe," Marion said as her mom drove up. But she wasn't so sure.

Meant to Bee

The next morning, Marion got settled at her desk in Mrs. Sienna's second-grade classroom. It was Monday. That meant they had science right before lunch.

"Today we'll learn about monarch butterflies," Mrs. Sienna told the class, and Marion immediately perked up.

Mrs. Sienna held up a diagram. It showed how a butterfly egg changed into a larva, or caterpillar. Then the caterpillar wrapped itself up and became a pupa. When it came out, it was a butterfly.

"Then the adult female monarchs lay more eggs," said Mrs. Sienna. "And the cycle starts again."

She told the class they could all work together on their classwork. They read a short handout about monarchs. Then they wrote down one fact for each stage of a monarch's life cycle.

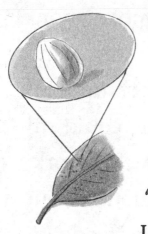

Marion read out a fact on eggs. "A monarch egg is no larger than the tip of a pencil!" She held up her pencil. "Wow! That's tiny."

Liz underlined a sentence about larvae. "A monarch larva eats only milkweed leaves," she read. "That's why milkweed is such an important plant. No milkweed, no monarchs!"

Ellie found a fact about the pupa. "The shell of a pupa starts off green with shiny golden dots. Then it changes to white. And then it becomes see-through."

Amy found the last fact about adult monarchs. "The butterfly comes out of the pupa in its adult size," said Amy. "It drinks nectar from flowers like clover and milkweed."

"More cheers for milkweed!" said Marion.

Before lunch, Mrs. Sienna passed out copies of a flyer. Marion did a double take. It was the same flyer the girls had seen in the park! The butterfly release!

"My friend is organizing this event," Mrs. Sienna said. "She is looking for volunteers. So if anyone is interested, please let me know."

Then the lunch bell rang. Most students went to get their lunch boxes and line up at the door.

But Marion went right up to Mrs. Sienna's desk. She had thought about the butterfly release all last night and it seemed like fate that Mrs. Sienna had handed out flyers in class. She was *meant* to volunteer for this!

"I'd like to help out," Marion said to her teacher.

"Great!" Mrs. Sienna replied. "My friend, Ms. Campbell, is an educator at the Arboretum. She would love your help."

Marion thought back to the ladybug release at the Arboretum. The nice lady who was running the event had gently removed the lady-bug from Gabby's head. That is, *after* Gabby had stopped screaming.

"Was Ms. Campbell at the lady-bug release last year?" Marion asked.

Mrs. Sienna nodded. "Yes! Did you meet her? She was probably dressed as a ladybug."

Marion smiled. "Yes!" She remembered Ms. Campbell's ladybug-print dress and matching hat. She seemed really fun.

"I'll get all the details for you," Mrs. Sienna told Marion. "Ms. Campbell will be so grateful for your help! And so will the butterflies!"

Marion beamed and hurried to get in line for lunch.

Chapter 3

Save the Butterflies!

In the cafeteria, Marion and her friends sat down at a table near the windows.

Liz hurried off to the hot lunch line. "Veggie fried rice today! Yessss!" she said excitedly.

Marion laughed. Liz was vegan. The days when she could eat the school lunch were special.

"So what were you talking to Mrs. Sienna about?" Ellie asked Marion.

Marion was still holding the flyer. "The butterfly release," Marion replied. "I'm going to be a volunteer."

Amy studied the flyer more closely. "What *is* a butterfly release, anyway?" she asked.

"The people at the Arboretum raise the monarchs from eggs. Then the monarchs are released into the wild every summer. It helps boost their population," Marion explained.

Ellie finished chewing a bite of her sandwich. "What do the volunteers do?" Ellie asked.

Marion frowned. "I don't know yet," she replied. "Want to volunteer with me? We'll find out!"

Ellie looked at the date. She shook her head. "That night I'm going to see a musical with Nana Gloria."

"I wish I could volunteer," said Amy. "But that weekend I'm going to see my dad and stepmom and Chloe." Chloe was Amy's stepsister. They lived in Orange Blossom, the next town over.

Liz sat down with her lunch tray.

"How about you, Liz?" Marion asked. "Want to volunteer with me?" She showed Liz the flyer.

But Liz couldn't make it either. "Sorry," she said. "Camping trip."

Marion frowned. She hadn't thought she'd be volunteering *alone*.

"Hey, what about Gabby?" Liz suggested.

Marion thought for a moment. What were the chances her bug-phobic sister would want to do it?

There was only one way to find out.

Chapter 4

Too Much Bug Talk

That night, Marion walked into the kitchen after finishing her home-work. Her dad was making pasta and her favorite tomato sauce. It was sweet and a tiny bit spicy.

Marion peeked inside the pot. Her dad gave it a stir. "Almost ready," he said. "How about you and Gabby set the table?"

Gabby went around and put a napkin at each place. Marion followed with the forks. Gabby put out the glasses. Marion filled a water pitcher.

Then Marion's mom came in from their home office. "Mmm, that smells so good!" she exclaimed. She helped serve the pasta.

Soon all four of them were sitting down to dinner. Marion passed around the grated cheese.

"So how was everyone's day?" Mrs. Ballard asked.

Gabby described a craft she'd made in her kindergarten class.

"We started a new unit in science," Marion told them. "Did you know that monarch butterflies fly south for the winter? Some of them travel more than two thousand miles!"

"Whoa!" said Gabby. "They must be tired when they get there!"

Marion went on to tell them about the butter- fly release. "Mrs. Sienna said they need volunteers," she said. "I told her I'd help."

Mrs. Sienna had given Marion more details at the end of the day. All the volunteers would need to come for training. They would learn what to do the day of the event. "Training is this Saturday," Marion said. "And then the butterfly release is the week after."

Marion's parents nodded at each other. "Sounds great!" said her mom.

"I'm happy to drive you," said her dad.

"Thanks!" said Marion with a smile.

Then she turned to Gabby. "Doesn't it sound like fun?" she asked Gabby. "Do you want to volunteer too? To help the butterflies?"

But Gabby cringed and leaned back in her chair. "Butterflies? Ewwww! No way!"

Marion sighed. "Oh, come on, Gabby," she said. "They're colorful. And gentle. They don't sting. How can you be afraid of butterflies?"

Gabby took a big bite of pasta. She couldn't say anything. So she just shook her head and closed her eyes.

"But butterflies are small," Marion went on. "Think of how huge *you* look to *them*."

Gabby's face was starting to turn red.

"They're way more afraid of you than you are of them." Marion tried to convince her. "You should volunteer. You'll see. It'll be fun!"

Gabby pushed back her chair. She jumped up. "No, no, no!" she shouted. "I don't want to! I don't want to be near butterflies!" With that, she ran away from the table and up the stairs.

Marion started to go after her. "Gabby, wait!"

But her mom stopped her. "It's okay, Marion. Let her be for a bit. I think you hit a nerve."

"I'll say," Marion agreed, and sat back down.

Why couldn't her sister just relax when it came to bugs?

A Place for Trees

For the rest of the week, Marion tried not to talk about butterflies around Gabby. She wished she could change Gabby's mind. But she felt like she would just make it worse.

On Saturday, Marion's dad drove her to the Arboretum.

"Did you know that *arboretum*

means
'a place for
trees' in Latin?"
Marion said to her dad.

Marion loved the Arboretum. It was home to so many different trees and plants. Many of the trees were labeled. Little signs at their bases listed the types of trees and the years they were planted.

Birch

Maple

"Mrs. Sienna said to meet Ms. Campbell on the West Lawn," Marion said. She had printed out a map.

They drove past a large greenhouse. The map showed it as the Potting Shed.

They drove by a field of orange and yellow lilies. "The Lily Garden!" said Marion.

They passed rows of prickly hollies shaped like Christmas trees. "Those must be the Holly Beds. So up ahead is the West Lawn."

Sure enough, they came to an open grassy area. Marion saw a check-in table with a sign that said VOLUNTEERS. A tall woman stood behind the table. She was dressed in a butterfly-print dress. A butterfly headband held back her long silver hair.

Marion recognized Ms. Campbell right away.

Mr. Ballard parked the car. Then Marion walked with him to the check-in table. Ms. Campbell greeted them warmly and asked Marion's dad to fill out some forms. She reminded him when pick-up was. Then he drove off with a wave.

"Well, Marion," said Ms. Campbell. "I was so excited when Ruth told me you wanted to volunteer."

Ruth? thought Marion. Oh! Mrs. Sienna's first name was Ruth. It was funny to hear someone call her that.

"In fact, Ruth says you are a star in the classroom," Ms. Campbell went on.

Marion beamed. She loved school, and she had to admit that it felt pretty great to be called a star.

Ms. Campbell showed Marion around. She introduced her to the other volunteers. Many were older kids, but a few were around Marion's age.

Four of the volunteers were making dioramas. "I'll use them in my presentation on the day of the butterfly release," Ms. Campbell explained to Marion. "Each one will show a different stage of the monarch's life cycle: egg, larva, pupa, and butterfly!"

Some other volunteers were fixing holes in a dome of white netting. "The butterflies will be in here before we release them," Ms. Campbell said.

A few people were making paper chain garlands. "We'll use these as decorations on the big day," Ms. Campbell said.

Marion looked around. All the volunteers had something to do, except her. "What can I help with?" Marion asked.

Ms. Campbell smiled. "I have one very important job left," she said.

Marion in Charge

Ms. Campbell led Marion to a table near the diorama-makers.

On the table there were boxes of markers and crayons. There was a pile of regular glue and glitter glue tubes. And there was a package of extra-large paper in a variety of rainbow colors.

Under the table there was a

box with ribbons, tissue paper, and cardboard.

Marion's eyes lit up. "Is this a craft table?" she asked excitedly.

Ms. Campbell nodded. "Something for event participants to make and take home to remember the day," she said with a smile. "What do you think?"

"I think it's a great idea!" Marion replied. "What kind of craft will it be?"

Ms. Campbell pointed out some project ideas on the table. One showed how to make butterfly wings to wear like a backpack. Another showed a butterfly headband project.

"Like the one you're wearing!" Marion said. She pointed at Ms. Campbell's hair. "Did you make it?"

Ms. Campbell laughed. "Yes! I thought it could be a good project.

I brought some plain headbands to use." She pointed to the box under the table. "But you decide. You're in charge!"

Wow! Marion thought. Just her? In charge of the whole craft table? She felt so important.

Ms. Campbell had an idea. "Whatever craft you choose, why don't you test it out first? That way we can make sure it's fun and easy, even for the younger kids."

Marion agreed. "I'll get started right away!"

She decided to try making a butterfly headband like Ms. Campbell's.
She traced a butterfly shape onto an orange piece of paper.
She carefully cut it out.

Then she picked out a black marker. She added markings to the orange wings. Now it *sort of* looked like a monarch butterfly.

Finally, she glued the butterfly to a plain headband.

Marion tried on the headband and looked in the handheld mirror on the table. The headband had been easy to make. And it was definitely fun. It didn't look *exactly* like a monarch, but it was only her first try.

Now she just needed to test out the butterfly wing project, and the craft table would be ready to go!

71

A Butterfly Joke

On the way home, Marion's dad admired her headband.

"Thanks!" said Marion. "But I can't figure out why it doesn't look exactly like a monarch," she admitted. "And I want to make sure this craft turns out *perfect*."

"I think we have some nature books at home," said her dad.

"Maybe you could take a look and see if you can find a photo of a monarch."

"Good idea!" said Marion excitedly.

At home, she scanned the books on the bookshelf. "Aha!" she suddenly exclaimed.

She pulled out a big hardcover called *Butterflies of the World*. Inside were beautiful full-color photos— of maybe every type of butterfly in the world. *That's why it's so heavy!* Marion thought.

Marion found a monarch butterfly photo.

She held her headband up next to it. She knew what to do.

Marion was working so hard that she didn't hear the doorbell. She jumped a little when Ellie appeared at her side.

"What are you doing?" Ellie asked Marion.

Marion was sitting at the dining room table. She was cutting up an orange piece of paper. In front of her, the big butterfly book was open to the monarch page.

"Hi!" Marion exclaimed. "I'm making a butterfly headband!"

She explained to Ellie how she was going to be in charge of the craft table at the butterfly release.

"Want to make one?" Marion asked.

Ellie's eyes lit up. "Sure!" she replied. Ellie dropped into the seat next to Marion.

Marion handed her orange paper and a pair of scissors.

They both cut out their butterflies. Then Marion passed Ellie a marker. She showed Ellie the monarch photo.

"The black markings look like this," Marion said.

She drew stripes and long looping lines—just as they looked in the photo.

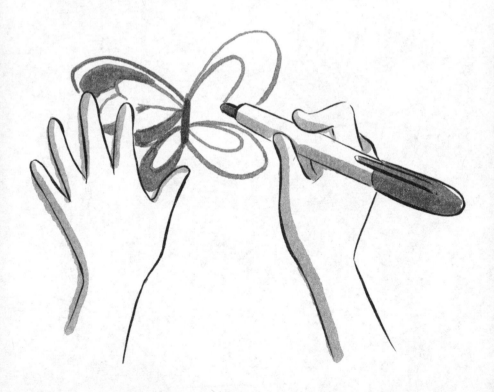

"And see those white dots?" Marion said. She opened a tube of white paint she had found in the art drawer. Marion dabbed them on the wings with a paintbrush.

Ellie did everything just as Marion did.

Then Gabby strolled in from the kitchen. "Can I make one?" she asked.

"Sure!" Marion replied. "But I thought you didn't like butterflies," she said, her eyes narrowed.

"I don't like *real* ones," said Gabby. "I like paper ones!"

Marion smiled. "Here," she said. "I'll show you how to make one."

Marion passed Gabby an orange piece of paper. But Gabby reached for an aqua one.

"Don't you want to make a *monarch* butterfly?" Marion asked her.

Gabby shook her head. "No thanks," she said.

When it was time to add markings, Gabby used red and orange
and green markers. It was a beautiful rainbow creation. It definitely
didn't look like a monarch, but
Marion decided not to say anything. She was just glad her sister
had decided to join them.

All three of them glued
their butterflies onto
headbands. Then
they tried them on.

"Yours looks
great!" Ellie told
Gabby.

"You may not have liked a lady-bug on your head, but just look at the giant *butterfly* on your head!" Marion said.

All three girls laughed, and Marion was glad that Gabby could at least *joke* about butterflies now.

Chapter 8

The Big Day

All week long, Marion prepared for the butterfly release.

She asked her mom to make color copies of the monarch photo so she could scatter them around the craft table. She gathered up all the black markers in the house. She even got the art store in town to donate extra orange paper.

Marion also practiced the other craft, the backpack butterfly wings. They turned out great! But she knew she would need more cardboard for that project. She took some from the recycling bin in the garage.

On the big day, Marion was excited. Well, mostly excited. But also a little nervous. Was she ready? Would the visitors like the craft table? Marion asked her mom to drop her off at the Arboretum early. She needed time for last-minute preparations.

Once there, she organized the markers, tidied the paper, and unpacked all the extras she'd brought from home.

Then she put on the butter-fly headband and wings she had made. She thought they'd come in handy to show as examples!

Finally, visitors started to arrive. *Here we go!* thought Marion.

"Welcome to the butterfly release!" Ms. Campbell called out. Everyone gathered around. "Monarch butterflies are beautiful and amazing," she began.

Marion's ears perked up as Ms. Campbell mentioned some monarch facts Marion already knew and used the dioramas to show the life cycle of a monarch.

"But monarchs are just one kind of pollinator," Ms. Campbell went on. "And most of the world's flowering plants need a pollinator. Otherwise they can't reproduce."

Marion could not imagine a world without flowering plants.

"We'll have our butterfly release in half an hour," Ms. Campbell said. "In the meantime, feel free to look around. We've set up a games station, a meet-a-butterfly station, and an arts and crafts station."

That was Marion's cue. She took her spot at the craft table. She was ready for the crafters. But would they come?

Within minutes, Marion's table was crowded with kids.

"Hello!" she said cheerily. She explained the two projects— headband or wings—and got everyone started. "I'm here if you need help!" she added.

All around her, kids were reaching for art supplies. Marion turned one way to pass the scissors. She turned the other way to open the glue. She reached under the table for ribbon to make wing straps.

It was hard to keep track of everything.

Before Marion knew it, one girl was gluing a *purple* butterfly onto a headband. Oh no! It didn't look like a monarch.

And a boy was trying on blue polka-dotted wings. That definitely didn't look like a monarch!

Then some glue spilled. A small child was crying that he ripped his butterfly.

Plus everyone was using all kinds of colors and crazy patterns!

Marion didn't know what to do!

Then Marion felt a tap on her shoulder. She turned around.

"Ellie!" Marion cried. "You came!"

Ellie smiled and nodded. "The music concert was postponed," she told Marion. "So Nana Gloria brought me here. And I brought someone with me."

Ellie stepped to one side. Someone shorter was stand-ing right behind her. It was Gabby!

"Can we help?" Gabby asked.

Chapter 9

Surprise Guests

Marion was so relieved to see them. "Yes! Thank you! I could use the help," Marion told them.

She pulled Ellie to the side. "They're not following the directions," she whispered. "These don't look like monarch butterflies!"

Ellie looked around the craft table. Then she looked back at

Marion, confused. "I think they look great!" Ellie said.

Marion opened her mouth to object. But just at that moment, a bumblebee buzzed among all three girls. It buzzed up against the sunflower on Gabby's T-shirt.

"Eeeep!" Gabby shrieked. She closed her eyes. She clenched her fists down by her sides. "Get it away, get it away, please!"

Marion sprang into action. "Gabby, it's okay!" she said. "Stay calm." Marion gently shooed the bumblebee away. Soon it was buzzing around a nearby camellia bush.

Gabby opened her eyes. She took a deep breath.

"Wow," Marion said. "You didn't run around screaming or anything. Not like when the ladybug was on your head."

"Well, the bee wasn't on my head!" Gabby replied. "But that was still kind of scary."

Suddenly Marion had a flash-back. Why hadn't she thought of this before?

"You know, Gabby," Marion said, "I was kind of afraid of some frogs at The Critter Club once."

Gabby looked surprised. "Really?" she asked.

Ellie nodded. "I remember that!" She turned to Gabby. "One frog got out of the tank. Your sister did *not* like that."

Gabby laughed a little. "Yep," said Marion. "But after a while, once I got used to the frogs and learned more about them, I real- ized they're actually really cool animals. So maybe if you try to remember that bees and butter- flies mostly do great things for the world, then you won't be so nervous about them."

Gabby was quiet for a moment. Then she nodded. "Maybe," Gabby said.

Together, the girls stepped back up to the craft table.

"*You* shouldn't be so nervous either," Ellie said to Marion.

Marion frowned. "About what?" she asked.

"About this," Ellie said. She pointed to the busy crafters. A three-year-old was scribbling on her butterfly wings. A boy was covering his wings in black tissue paper. A girl had decided to put only antennae on her headband.

"Everyone's will be different," Ellie said. "But that's the beauty of the craft!"

Ellie was right. Marion had been nervous that the crafts wouldn't look good. And that Ms. Campbell would think she'd made a mistake putting Marion in charge.

Now, looking around, Marion saw that the craft table was a hit. It was crowded. Everyone was having fun. Kids and grown-ups walked around wearing their wings and headbands. Everyone's crafts *did* look different. And they were all beautiful!

Up, Up, and Away

Ms. Campbell's voice rang out from the butterfly dome.

"We're ready for the butterfly release!" she announced.

Cheers went up all around the West Lawn. Visitors of all ages gathered around the dome.

At the craft table, Marion and Gabby capped all the markers and glue tubes. Then they rushed to the dome too.

It was Marion's first chance to see it filled with monarch butterflies. There were so many! Too many to count. Especially because they wouldn't stay still. They fluttered this way and that. Some of them bumped into one another.

"Just think about how many plants they will pollinate!" Marion said.

Ms. Campbell and another Arboretum worker stood next to the net flaps. "On the count of three, we'll open these flaps. Then our butterfly friends will start their life in the wild. Everyone, count with me!"

Marion and Gabby looked at each other. They counted along with the crowd. "One . . . two . . . three!"

The net flaps opened. The butterflies streamed up and out. Everyone clapped and cheered.

Many butterflies flew up, up, up into the clear blue sky.

Others flew into nearby trees and shrubs.

A few fluttered in and among the crowd of people. One flew right in front of Ellie's nose. It circled Marion's head. Then it landed on Marion's shoulder!

"Look!" Marion said in a whisper. She didn't want to scare the butterfly away.

Next to Marion, Gabby stared at the butterfly. Then she looked into Marion's eyes. A smile spread slowly across Gabby's face.

"It *is* very cool," Gabby admitted.

Ellie nudged Gabby. "Maybe one will land on you!" she whispered.

Gabby shook her head. "No, that's okay."

Marion laughed. "We'll take some more baby steps before we have you holding a bug," she said.

The butterfly took flight, and the three girls watched as it flew up and away into the clear blue sky.

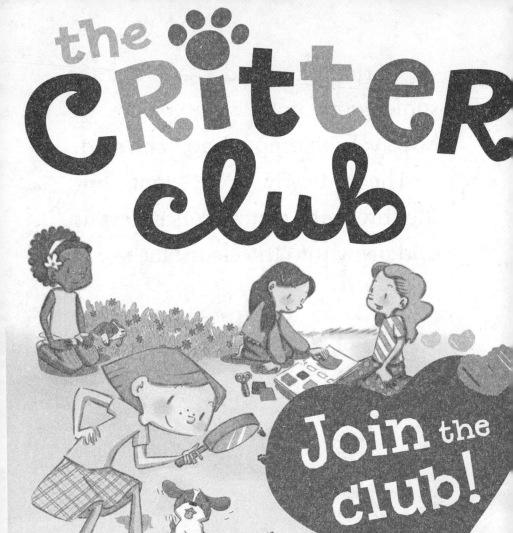